"HOW COME YOU'RE NOT LAUGHING?"

"You're always laughing," Phil said. How come you're not laughing now?"

"Because I don't feel like it, Phil. Because you're not very funny. But I'll tell you something, Phil...just leave me alone. I like sitting in the shade by myself, and not being made a fool of."

"Who made a fool of you?"

"You did, Phil. You made a fool of me. And you made a fool of yourself, too. Nobody likes to be used. And that's what you were doing with me..."

Other Avon Flare Books by
Marilyn Sachs

CLASS PICTURES

MARILYN SACHS says, "One of the happiest romances of my life began on a beach when I was seventeen. I haven't forgotten, which is why I wrote BEACH TOWELS."

Mrs. Sachs has also written CLASS PICTURES. She lives in San Francisco.

Beach Towels

MARILYN SACHS

Illustrated by
JIM SPENCE

AN AVON FLARE BOOK

with love to Pauline Smith

AVON BOOKS
A division of
The Hearst Corporation
1790 Broadway
New York, New York 10019

Published by arrangement with E.P. Dutton, Inc.
Library of Congress Catalog Card Number: 82-5056
ISBN: 0-380-68825-5

Library of Congress Cataloging in Publication Data

Sachs, Marilyn. Beach towels.

Summary: Two teenagers get to know each other better and better during the weeks they share the shade of a tree on the beach.
[1. Friendship—Fiction]
I. Spence, Jim, ill. II. Title.
PZ7.S1187Bd [Fic] 82-5056
AACR2

First Flare Printing, July, 1984

WFH 10 9 8 7 6 5 4 3 2 1

Tuesday

"Excuse me," Lori said. "Would you mind moving over?"

No answer.

"Excuse me." She raised her voice. "I'm sorry to bother you. Would you mind just moving over a little bit?"

"What?" The boy opened his eyes.

"I'm sorry. I guess I woke you up. I didn't know you were asleep."

Lori smiled at him, but he didn't smile back. His forehead wrinkled, and he looked angry.

"What do you want?" he asked in a grumpy voice. He sat up on his towel. It was a green, yellow and red striped one.

"If you wouldn't mind moving over just a little bit, I could put my towel down."

"Why does it have to be here?" he asked. "There's plenty of room on the beach."

"Because the shade is here. I have to sit in the shade. I get a bad sunburn if I stay out in the sun too long."

"Well, why don't you go over there, on the other side of the beach? There's plenty of shade there. We're packed in like sardines here."

"Because it's too close to the rest rooms over there," Lori explained. "You can smell them. All you have to do is just move over a little bit."

He made an angry sound. But he stood up and tugged at his towel. Lori noticed he was tall. Even taller than she was, and she was five feet ten inches.

"Thanks a lot," she told him, and flashed a big smile. But he turned his back and didn't look at her.

She laid her towel down on the sand. All of it didn't fit because it was so crowded there under the big tree. You had to be careful how you moved, or you might step on someone. She put down her radio and her bag of lunch. Then she slipped out of her jeans and her shirt. She yanked at the bottom of her bathing suit. It kept riding up her rear end. Maybe she had gained some weight this past month. Finally she sat down. Her towel was red with blue and white stars. She sat down on a white star.

"Excuse me."

The boy was standing over her. He had to climb over her towel to get out. Because of the way she had put her towel down, there was no room for him to walk around.

"Oh, sure!"

He stepped over her towel and began walking across the beach towards the refreshment stand. Lori watched him. He was very tall. Maybe six three or even six four. He had a nice tan, too. Not bad looking.

She put her radio on and listened to Blondie. She could see the boy over near the refreshment stand. He wasn't buying anything. He was using the phone. She watched him as he walked back across the sand. She guessed the hot sand was burning his feet because he kind of hopped, and he looked angry when he returned.

"Excuse me."

"Oh, sure!"

She flipped to another station and listened to Queen. She swayed a little to the music and looked over towards the lake. It was very blue and sparkling. The sky was blue, and the people were little spots of color inside all that blue. She felt relaxed.

"Hey—will you turn that down!"

"What?"

"I said will you stop that racket!" the boy shouted. "You've got some nerve."

"Okay. You don't have to get so excited."

"And you don't have to break my eardrums either. I came here for a little peace and quiet, and I can't even hear myself think."

"Because you're shouting so loud." Lori couldn't help smiling. "You're the one who's making all the noise."

"You people really have a lot of nerve."

"What people?"

"You people with radios," the boy yelled. "I bet you take it everywhere you go. On buses, on trains, to the ball park, to the library . . ."

"I don't take it to the library. I don't even go to the library."

"Don't you ever think that other people may not want to listen to that junk? Don't you ever think of anybody else?"

"You're the one who's complaining. Nobody else minds," Lori told him, but she turned down the volume.

"You can't hear what anybody is saying."

"But nobody is saying anything except you." Lori smiled.

"I'm expecting a friend, and I'd like to be able to talk to her when she comes."

"If she's got a voice as loud as yours, you won't have any trouble hearing her." Lori started laughing.

He was being such a jerk. And she liked the way she had told him off. She felt proud of herself.

Sometimes when people said mean things, she didn't know what to say back to them. Sometimes she didn't say anything. She just stood there and took it and felt foolish. Then later she thought of all the smart things she should have said.

But today she sure had come up with a good one. "If she's got a voice as loud as yours, you won't have any trouble hearing her." Boy, that was a good one!

She laughed so hard she couldn't stop. She had to put her head down over her knees. She turned her back to the boy, and she kept on laughing for a long time.

Wednesday

The boy was already there, his towel spread out in the shade under the big tree. It was the best spot—right in the middle of the shade. He looked up and made a face when he saw her. A mean, angry face. Was that the way he always looked?

She moved off as far away from him as she could but still in the shade. After she had spread out her beach towel, she sat down on it and flipped on her radio. Not very loud, but not very low either. Then she looked over at him. There was something about him. He looked familiar. Suddenly it came to her.

"Hey!" she called. "Hey!"

"What?"

"Do you work at Sugar Daddy's?"

"What?"

"I said do you work at Sugar Daddy's?" she repeated.

"Oh! I can hardly hear you with that thing blasting away."

"I said . . ."

"I know what you said. Yeah, I do work at Sugar Daddy's."

Lori lowered the volume. She grinned at the boy. "You waited on me last week. Let me see—I guess it was on Tuesday."

"I don't work on Tuesday."

"Maybe it was Wednesday. At night. About eight."

"Could be," the boy said. "I work the late shift—from four to nine."

"Yes, it was Wednesday. I was there with my girl friend, Joanie Summers. It was you. You told us to try the Irish coffee ice cream."

"I don't remember."

"Sure—you were the one. Joanie was going to order mango, and I wanted butter pecan, but you said we should try the Irish coffee. You said it was the best flavor. You were real nice."

"That's the only decent flavor."

"And you gave us both double scoops, even

though we only paid for single scoops. You were real nice."

His face wasn't so mean looking anymore. He wasn't exactly smiling but nearly.

"Don't you remember? Joanie gave you a five-dollar bill, and you made believe you were going to keep the change. Like it was a tip. You were only kidding. Then your boss came out, and you made such a funny face behind his back that the two of us burst out laughing. And you were laughing too. Then he turned around. . . ."

"Oh yeah—I remember." Now he was smiling. Really smiling.

"You were real nice."

"He's a nerd, my boss," he said.

"He looks like a nerd."

"He's always trying to act like nobody does anything unless he's there to lean on them. When he's around, nothing gets done right. Friday, he folded up some cartons to put the ice cream in, and all the bottoms fell out. We get twice as much work done when he's not around."

Lori laughed. The boy smiled and nodded. They looked at each other and then he said, "Well . . ." She waited, but he didn't say anything after that. So she began flipping the knobs on her radio. The next time she looked over at him he was reading.

She stood up. "Uh—say—would you mind watching my things? I think I'm going to take a swim now."

"Okay."

"I've got my wallet inside my jeans, and I'm leaving my watch inside my sandals." Lori pointed to the pile on her beach towel.

"Well, don't yell it all over the beach."

"I'm not yelling."

"Okay—go ahead. I'll watch. Go ahead, but turn off your radio first."

Lori laughed. She turned off the radio. Then she walked across the sand to the water. Even though it was only eleven, the sand felt warm. In another hour, it would really be hot.

She dived right in, head first, and shivered as the water closed over her head. She began to swim very quickly, and suddenly she wasn't cold anymore. She swam out beyond the raft, and she heard the lifeguard blow his whistle. He didn't have to worry about her. She was a strong swimmer.

She laughed as she heard him announce on the loudspeaker, "Please do not swim out past the raft. Do not swim out past the raft. . . ."

After a while, she turned around and swam back. When she reached the raft, she climbed up on it and stretched out. Only for a few minutes. The sun felt good, but she had to be careful. Her skin was so fair that she could only stay out in the sun a few minutes at a time when the summer began. After a while, when her tan built up, she could stay out longer.

When she came out of the water, she stood for a few minutes in the sun until she was all dripped off.

"Thanks," she told the boy when she returned to her beach towel.

"You really swam far out," he said. "The lifeguard was sore."

Lori grinned. "He always gets sore."

The boy looked at her in a funny way. "Looks like you're good at it—making people sore."

Lori laughed.

"And laughing. You sure laugh a lot."

"Why not? It's better to laugh than to cry."

"Did you ever try just doing nothing?" asked the boy.

"What?"

"I mean not laughing, not crying, not bothering people, not making them sore—just doing nothing."

She didn't answer his question. She laughed

and told him, "If you want to go swimming, I'll watch your things."

"Thanks, but I'm waiting for someone."

"Your friend."

"That's right," he said quickly.

"Did she come yesterday?"

"No, she . . . she couldn't make it. But she's coming today. Before lunch. She said around eleven."

Lori picked up her watch. "It's eleven thirty," she told him. He didn't say anything. They didn't talk to each other anymore that day. At three o'clock he got up, rolled up his towel and left. She guessed he was going to work. His friend had never showed.

Thursday

"Hey, you—what time is it?" the boy asked.

"It's twelve thirty."

"Thanks. My watch stopped."

Lori figured he must have arrived at the beach before anybody else. His red, green and yellow striped beach towel was spread out right in the center of the shade. It stayed shady in that spot all through the day. The shade moved around in the other places.

She had put her red towel with the blue and white stars not far from his. She would have to move it later as the sun moved. He was frowning down at his watch. She couldn't help laughing. He heard her and looked at her in a mean way.

"Uh—what's your name, anyway?" she said, and tried to stop laughing.

"Phil."

He didn't ask her what her name was. She told him anyway.

"My name is Lori, Lori Fisher. I go to Kennedy High School. Where do you go?"

"Berkeley High."

"I'm a junior."

No answer.

"I'm a junior," Lori told him. "What are you?"

"Oh! I'm a senior. I mean if I decide to go back, I'll be a senior."

"What do you mean?"

"I mean," he said very slowly, "that I just may drop out of school. Any more questions?"

"Yeah," she said, laughing. "How come you sit in the shade all the time? You've got a great tan, and your skin is dark. Why don't you sit out in the sun?"

"Because my friend likes the shade."

"Your friend? Oh, you mean the one who never comes?"

As soon as she said it, Lori was sorry. She hadn't meant to hurt his feelings. She guessed he was waiting for the girl again today. And she also guessed that the girl would stand him up again.

She laughed nervously and said, without looking at him, "Well, I guess it's lunchtime." She unwrapped her sandwich and took a bite.

"I'm really starving," she said, trying to say something unimportant. Something that wouldn't make him feel bad. What did she have to go and make him feel bad for?

"I always get hungry at noon," she went on. "Even if I've eaten breakfast at eleven, I'm still hungry at twelve. It's like there's a clock inside my belly. Mmm! This is good. What have you got for lunch?"

"Nothing."

"Aren't you hungry?"

"I guess so. I was going to buy lunch. I was just waiting until . . . until later."

Lori guessed he was planning to wait until his friend came.

"Here," she said, "take a half of my sandwich. I can't eat it. Really, I can't."

"No." He shook his head, but he was looking at the half of sandwich she held out.

"Go ahead and take it."

"No—I can wait."

"Go ahead. It's really too much for me."

"Is it egg salad?"

"Uh huh."

"I like egg salad." He was still looking at the sandwich.

"So do I. I eat it every day."

"Every day?"

"Uh huh. It makes me feel good." Lori laughed.

"Maybe you should eat something else. You laugh so much, maybe it makes you feel too good."

But he took the sandwich.

"This is great."

"See—it's going to make you feel good, too."

"It's marvelous," he said. "It's the best egg salad sandwich I ever tasted. What have you got in it?"

"If I told you, you wouldn't want to eat it."

"I just want to know what's in it. I never tasted egg salad that was so good."

"You won't think so if I tell you."

"Come on."

"Okay—well, there's hard-boiled egg," Lori said.

"No kidding!"

"And green onion."

"Okay."

"And mayonnaise," she went on.

"So far so good."

"And salt and pepper."

"No problem."

"And . . ." Lori stopped.

"And?"

"You sure you want to know?"

"I'm sure," he said.

"Maybe you ought to finish eating before I tell you."

"Okay—one last swallow. There. I'm finished. So what's the secret ingredient?"

"Peanut butter," she told him.

"Peanut butter? You've got to be kidding."

"No, I mean it. But it has to be the crunchy kind. The kind with nuts."

"I hate peanut butter." He made a face.

"See, I told you you wouldn't like it."

"But it tasted wonderful."

Lori unwrapped some cookies and held one out to him.

"Here, have a cookie."

"What's in it? Lighter fluid?"

"No, I didn't make them. They're just chocolate chip cookies from the store."

"Thanks."

"And here—you can have half of my peach."

"Okay, but I'll buy you a drink," Phil said. "What do you like?"

"You don't have to."

"It's okay. I want to. What do you like?"

"Lime frosties," Lori answered.

"I don't think they have lime. Only Coke or root beer frosties."

"Well, I'll take root beer then. But ask them if they have lime first."

She watched him half hop, half run across the sand. You really needed to wear shoes when it got this hot. He went over to the phone before he went to the refreshment stand. She watched him as he dialed. The call lasted about ten minutes.

After he hung up, he headed for the refreshment stand. When he returned, he handed her a root beer frostie. He also handed her a hot dog.

"I decided to buy a couple of hot dogs," he said.

"But I didn't want one."

"You gave me half of your lunch. I figured you'd still be hungry."

She was still hungry. There was mustard and relish on the hot dog, too. Just the way she liked it. She took a bite and laughed. "Thanks. I am still hungry, I guess. That's a big problem of mine. I'm usually hungry."

"You're a big girl."

"I'm not that big."

"I mean you're tall and—well, you're a big girl. I'm pretty big myself, and I think I get hungrier than a lot of my friends."

"I'm not that big."

"Look, I didn't mean to hurt your feelings. You look okay—not fat or anything. Girls always get touchy if you say anything about their bodies."

Lori laughed. "I guess we're never satisfied. All my life I've wanted to be little. I'm five ten and I weigh— Well, never mind what I weigh. But I always wanted to be little and skinny and flat-chested."

The boy looked her over quickly. Not with any special interest. Like when you're shopping for a can of soup. You pick one, but you look at the other cans. That's how he was looking at her.

"You're not so big," he said finally. "But my friend, Ronda, she's kind of short. Maybe five two or five three. And very small-boned. She always says she wishes she was tall. She wants to be a model, and she says you have to be at least five seven to be a model."

"That's for me then."

"But you have to be skinny. Models starve themselves. You look fatter in a photo. So that's why they starve themselves. They have to be thinner than what they look like in a photo."

Lori laughed and took another bite out of her hot dog. "You just talked me out of it."

But he wasn't really listening to her. He was thinking about his friend.

"Ronda thinks she might become an airplane stewardess if she can't be a model. You don't have to be tall to be a stewardess."

"You don't even have to be a girl. You can be a guy nowadays. And they don't call them stewardesses anymore, either. They're flight attendants."

"Ronda likes to travel. She says if you work for an airline, you can go all over the world."

"Who's Ronda? Is she your friend who . . . I mean . . ."

"I just called her," Phil explained. "She thought she could get over to the beach today, but it didn't work out. She's looking for a summer job, and she had to go for an interview this morning. That's what she said. She felt bad. She really did. And she's definitely coming tomorrow."

"That's good."

The boy finished his hot dog and gathered up

his things. "Well, I guess I'll go sit in the sun now. See you around . . . uh . . ."

"Lori," she told him, "Lori Fisher."

"That's right. See you around, Lori. And thanks for the food."

Friday

"You've got a new beach towel, Phil."

"Uh . . . yeah . . . hi, Lori . . . yeah. I thought maybe I needed a new one."

"What was the matter with the old one?"

"Nothing was the matter with the old one. But it was old and looked kind of ratty and . . ."

"I liked it," she said. "I thought it was neat."

Lori spread her red beach towel with the blue and white stars down on the sand near Phil's. His new beach towel was bright yellow with orange and purple diamonds. She guessed he wanted to impress Ronda.

"Well, I like this one better. I had that old

one for a couple of years. Anyway, I got tired of it. Don't you get tired of things?"

"Not me," Lori told him. "I've had this beach towel for five years, and I never get tired of it. My mother . . . she . . . she used to tell me to get a new one. But I don't want a new one. I like it. I like all my old things. I don't want to change things."

"Well, life gets pretty dull if nothing changes."

"Maybe I like it dull. Maybe I don't want it to change. If I like something, I want to keep it that way."

"Like eating egg salad sandwiches every day?" he said.

"Yes—like eating egg salad sandwiches every day."

"No kidding, Lori, do you really eat an egg salad sandwich every day?"

"If I can, I do."

"For how long? I mean, how long have you been eating egg salad sandwiches?"

"Oh, only seven or eight months," she said.

"Only?"

"Well, before that I liked sardine and cream cheese sandwiches. I ate sardine and cream cheese sandwiches for about three years."

"Three years? Every day for three years?" He made a face.

"Sometimes I had to eat something else. If I was over at somebody else's house, or on a picnic, or out to lunch with my . . . with somebody. Sometimes I ate hamburgers or hot dogs. But I only really wanted sardines and cream cheese."

"My god!"

"And before that, when I was in elementary school, I ate peanut butter and jelly sandwiches."

"For how long?"

"For as long as I can remember," she told him. "All of my life going backwards."

"You must be a real picky eater."

"No, I'm not. I like all kinds of food. But I like to eat the same things for lunch."

"How about breakfast, Lori?"

"I like to eat the same thing for breakfast, too."

"What do you eat for breakfast?"

"Soup. I like soup for breakfast. It doesn't matter what kind of soup it is, but that's what I like for breakfast."

"How about dinner? What do you eat for dinner?"

"Oh, anything. I'm not fussy about dinner. Only lunch and I guess breakfast. And I'm fussy about my beach towel, and my blanket. It's a pink plaid one. I've had it ever since I moved out of my crib into my bed. And I like my pillow cases, too. There are two of them. It was a set. My mother embroidered them for me the Christmas I was six. They have pink rabbits on them, red flowers, and my name, *Lori*, in green. I love those pillow cases. I'm glad there are two. When one is being washed, I have the other one. I don't think I could sleep if I didn't put my head down on one of those pillow cases."

"What do you do when you sleep away from home?"

"I usually take one of them with me."

"Hey, you know something?" he said.

"What?"

"You're really a nut."

Lori laughed. "I guess I am."

"One of these days those pillow cases are going to wear out. What are you going to do then? Did you ever think of that?"

Lori stopped laughing. She didn't say anything.

"Okay, I can see that was the wrong thing to say. I'm sorry."

"It's all right, Phil. Besides, I think you owed me one."

"What do you mean?"

"I made you feel bad yesterday."

"When was that?"

"When I said something about your friend Ronda not coming."

"Oh, that's okay. She's been tied up all week."

Lori didn't say anything.

"But she's coming today."

Lori remained silent.

"She said she'll be here before lunch. It's still early. Let's see. It's only eleven thirty. Am I right? What time have you got?"

"Eleven forty-five."

"Well, it's still early," he said. "She'll be here today."

"I hope she will."

"What do you mean 'hope'?"

"Just what I said. I hope she will."

"You don't think she's coming, do you?" His face looked angry again.

No answer.

"You don't even know her, and you think she's a louse."

"I didn't say she was a louse, Phil."

"But you think so. I can see you think so."

"I don't think anything, but . . ."

"Just because she didn't show the other day?"

"The other three days," said Lori. "What kind of friend is she to keep somebody waiting all week? You're right. I don't know her, but I can't figure out why she doesn't come if she says she's going to come."

"She's been busy. Tuesday her mother needed her around the house. Let's see—Wednesday . . . I think she had a stomach ache. Thursday I guess some friends dropped over. . . ."

"No. Thursday she went for a job interview," Lori told him.

"That's right. She went for a job interview. So why don't you just get off her back."

Lori stood up.

"Where are you going?"

"Swimming."

"You want me to watch your things?" he asked.

"Okay."

She could hear the lifeguard shouting at her through the loudspeaker when she swam out past the raft. It cheered her up. She began laughing.

When she climbed up on the raft, the sun

felt good. Her skin was growing tanner, so she lay on the raft for fifteen or twenty minutes. When she got back to her towel, it was twelve fifteen. Phil was sitting up. He was all alone.

"How was your swim?" he asked.

"Just great. Why don't you go?"

"No . . . I'm waiting."

Lori sighed. She sat down on her towel and unwrapped her lunch.

"I bet I know what you have for lunch."

"I bet you do. Here." She was holding out a sandwich towards him.

"No thanks, Lori."

"It's okay, Phil. Go on, take it."

"I'm going to eat later. Besides, it's not right to keep eating your lunch."

"It's not my lunch. I mean, I brought along an extra one. I made two sandwiches today," she said.

"You made two?"

"Uh huh." she nodded.

"How come?"

"Well, I figured since you liked egg salad, I might as well make an extra one for you. That way, I can have a whole one, and so can you."

"But I told you Ronda was coming."

"I know."

"You didn't believe she was?"

"Well . . ." She looked away.

"That's why you made another egg salad sandwich, Lori. Because you were so sure she wouldn't show. You don't even know her, but . . ."

"Look, don't start that business again. Do you want the sandwich or not?" she asked.

"I just told you."

"What did you tell me?"

"That I'm waiting for my friend, and you can take your lousy sandwich and . . ."

Lori began laughing. She unwrapped the sandwich and began eating it herself. But she was laughing so hard, tears came to her eyes and she choked on the first bite. Then she stole a quick little look at Phil. He was glaring at her. It made her laugh even harder. Then he smiled. Soon he was laughing, too.

"You're really some character, Lori. Do you know that?"

"Yeah, I know."

"How come you laugh so much?"

"I like to laugh."

"You must be one happy person," he said, shaking his head.

Lori took a bite of her sandwich.

"Is that offer still good?" He was looking at her sandwich now.

"Which offer?"

"The offer of the other egg salad sandwich."

Lori held it out to him. He smiled at her, put out his hand and then suddenly jumped up.

"There she is. There she is."

"There who is?"

"Ronda. There's Ronda. Hey, Ronda, over here!"

"Is that Ronda? The little one in the blue bikini?"

"Uh huh. Over here, Ronda! Over here!"

"Who's that with her?"

"Oh. I guess that's her friend, Amy. Yes, that's who it is—Amy Wright."

"Why isn't she coming over?"

"I don't know."

"Look. She's putting her towel down right there in the sun," Lori said.

"That's funny. I thought she liked the shade. I've been getting here early every day because I thought she liked the shade. But see. She's waving at me. She wants me to come over there. I'll go over and talk to her. I'll be right back."

"I'll watch your things."

Lori watched Phil scamper across the hot sand. Ronda was standing up over her beach towel—a big orange one. Phil stood next to her.

They looked funny together. He was so much taller than she. Why did tall boys always seem to like short girls? Why didn't short girls go for short guys? Sometimes Lori hated short girls.

Phil came back and began gathering up his things.

"She says she wants to sit in the sun today. She thinks she's getting a cold. I guess I'll go over and sit there with her. So long, Lori."

"So long, Phil."

Lori wasn't really that hungry, but she ate the second egg salad sandwich anyway.

Monday

"What happened to you this weekend, Phil?"

"I never come to the beach on Saturdays or Sundays. I have to work both days."

"That's tough."

"No, it isn't. I don't mind. It's busy on the weekend. I like it better when it's busy. The job is so boring, and it's worse when you have to stand around."

"If it's so boring, how come you work there?"

"Because I have to, Lori. I need the money, and that's the only job I was able to find this summer."

"I wouldn't work at a job I didn't like."

"When you need money, you work at anything you can get. It's a lousy job, and it pays a lousy wage, but I had no choice. You don't have to work. You can just lie around on the beach every day and say you wouldn't work at a boring job. You're lucky."

"I'm not so lucky," she said.

"I'll get something better in the fall. There's a guy who runs a TV shop on Solano. He says he might hire me in the fall. I'm pretty good with TV repair."

"What will you do about school?"

"I'll take the equivalency test. I'm sick of school, and I'm sick of living at home. If I get that job in the TV store, I'm moving out. And I'm dropping out of school."

"And if you don't?" she asked.

"I think I will."

"But if you don't?"

"I don't know," he said. "I don't want to think about it. This is only the beginning of August. I have another month before I have to start worrying. Anyway, I wanted to ask you something."

"What?"

"Well, Ronda's coming today."

"That's nice."

"What does that mean?" he said sharply.

"What does what mean?"

"The way you said 'That's nice.' You said it in a funny way. What did you mean?"

Lori laughed. "You know, you've really got a chip on your shoulder. What are you getting all excited about? I didn't say anything."

"Because she did come Friday," he insisted. "You saw her. She came."

"That's right. She came."

"So?"

"So—calm down, Phil. Don't get so excited."

"Anyway, she came. I don't know if you hung around most of the afternoon."

"I did . . . until five. After you left."

"Well, you could see lots of kids from Berkeley High showed up. There was her friend Amy, and later Amy's brother Bob, and then two of Ronda's girl friends, Carol and Sue . . . and some other friends. . . ."

"And a couple of kids with radios . . ." Lori laughed.

"I didn't notice. Anyway, most of them are coming back today so I thought maybe you'd like to join us."

"Me?"

"Sure, Lori, you! I should have asked you Friday. I felt bad I didn't."

"Well, thanks, Phil, but you know I have to be careful of the sun."

"You're beginning to get a tan."

"I know," she said. "Yesterday I stayed out in the sun for a whole hour. But I don't like to stay out too long. I don't think too much sun is good for you."

"You were here yesterday?"

"Uh huh. And Saturday, too. I looked for you, Phil. I forgot you had to work on weekends."

"Was . . . was Ronda here?"

"She wasn't yesterday."

"Was she here on Saturday?"

"Yes, she was."

"Was she . . . was she here with a lot of her friends?" he asked.

"No, not a lot."

"Well, how many?"

"I didn't count."

"Okay, Lori, forget it. Just forget it."

"Look, Phil, you want to know?"

"Yes, I do."

"Maybe you won't feel so good if you know. Like knowing about the peanut butter in the egg salad."

"Go on, tell me."

"She was here with that girl friend of hers."

"Oh, Amy, Amy Wright. She's a nice girl, Amy. That's okay." He sounded pleased.

"And . . ."

"And?"

"And two guys." Lori told him.

"Was one of them Amy's brother, Bob?"

"Tall guy with red hair?"

"That's the one."

"He has a radio?" Lori asked.

"I don't know about the radio."

"And another guy—shorter, with brown hair. He was with Ronda's friend."

"I don't know who that is."

"Look, Phil . . ."

"Forget it, Lori. Just forget it."

"You asked me, Phil. You wanted to know."

"Anyway, how about it, Lori?"

"How about what?"

"How about joining us when Ronda comes?"

"I don't know, Phil. I don't know any of them, and I don't want to stay out in the sun too long. They're all your friends."

"They're really Ronda's friends."

"Oh—I see."

"So? What do you say, Lori?"

"Okay, Phil, but not for long."

"Whatever you say, Lori."

"Meanwhile, I think I'll take a swim."

"Maybe I'll go with you."

"I need somebody to watch my things," she told him.

"Well, how about that woman over there with the two kids? She looks okay, doesn't she?"

Phil only swam out to the raft. He wasn't as good a swimmer as Lori, and she left him there while she swam on. She could hear the lifeguard's voice over the loudspeaker, and she felt good.

Today she felt strong and happy. She could easily swim across the lake and back. But the lifeguard's voice was growing nasty. She turned around and headed back to the raft. Phil was sitting there when she pulled herself up. He was looking back towards the beach.

"I think I see them," he said.

"Who?"

"Ronda and Amy."

"Oh!"

"And some others."

Lori stretched herself out on the raft and felt the water trickling off her.

"You're a real good swimmer, Lori."

"Mmm."

"Are you on the swim team in your school?"

"I used to be."

"You're not anymore?"

"No . . . I wasn't this past term. Maybe next term I will. . . . I don't know," she said.

"You like school?"

"It's okay."

"Lori."

"What?"

"We should be getting back."

She wanted to tell him not to be such a jerk. She wanted to say "Look, Phil, that girl doesn't care for you. Forget about her. She just doesn't care for you. Stop being a fool." But she didn't. She just laughed, sat up and said, "Okay."

They dived off the raft together and headed for the shore.

Tuesday

"Lori, what happened to you yesterday?"

"Nothing."

"Where did you disappear to?"

"I didn't disappear. I just went home."

"How come you went home?"

"Because I felt like going home." She put her towel down on the beach but didn't look at him.

"You never go home early. You're always here when I leave. I figured you're probably the last one to go. I figured you like to wait until the lifeguard throws you out. Until he yells at you over his loudspeaker."

"Ha! Ha!"

"You're not laughing, Lori. You're always laughing. How come you're not laughing?"

"Because I don't feel like it, Phil. Because you're not very funny."

"Okay, why don't you just level with me? You're angry. I know you're angry. I don't know why. Yesterday, I just went off to get some drinks, and when I came back, you'd disappeared. Nobody even saw you go."

Lori flipped her radio on and didn't bother answering.

"Why are you angry, Lori?"

"I'm not angry."

"Yes, you are."

"No, I'm not. . . . But I'll tell you something, Phil . . . just leave me alone. I like sitting here in the shade."

"But you're really beginning to get a nice tan now, Lori. A few more days in the sun . . ."

"I like sitting in the shade by myself, listening to my radio, and not being made a fool of."

"Who made a fool of you?"

Lori turned up the volume.

"I asked you who made a fool of you."

Lori turned off her radio and yelled at him. "You did, Phil. You made a fool of me. And you made a fool of yourself, too. Every time she played around with Bob, you tried to do the same thing with me. You pushed me around, threw sand at me, dragged me into the water,

and acted like you didn't see what she was doing. You were trying to make her jealous. But then when she said she wanted something to drink, you were the one who went running to get it. The whole thing was disgusting. I couldn't stand it anymore. That's why I went home."

Lori turned her radio on again. She was angry and panting from talking so fast. Phil didn't say anything. After a while she looked at him, and he was sitting there with a long face. The way he usually looked. Sort of mean and sore. She stopped feeling angry. Before she could help it, she started to laugh.

"Never mind," she said. "I didn't mean to make you feel bad. Let's just forget the whole thing."

"I don't want to forget it."

"So don't forget it."

"Because I guess I wasn't fair to you. I'm sorry, Lori. You're right. I was a jerk. She did make me feel bad, and I wanted to pay her back. I didn't think you'd mind. You're such a good-natured girl, such a . . ."

"I've got feelings, too, like anybody else."

". . . such a good sport. I thought . . ."

"Look, Phil, nobody likes to be used. And that's what you were doing with me. I guess you didn't realize it. I guess you were feeling too lousy to think about anybody else. . . ."

"You're right. I was feeling lousy."

"So let me give you a piece of advice. Like I'm your mother." Lori laughed. "That girl's not for you. Forget about her. Can't you see the way she flirts with every boy in sight except you? The way she shakes all her movable parts for every male who comes near her except you? She's not interested in you. Can't you see?"

"She *is* interested in me. She's been interested in me for over a year."

"She's certainly got a great way of showing it."

"You don't understand. It's hard to explain. But she really likes me. . . . She . . . loves me."

"Phil, you're dreaming."

"No, listen. I never noticed her much until about six months ago. I was going around with a girl named Lisa Jackson, and Ronda was going around with a guy named Hank Fuller. We'd go out together sometimes, because the girls were friends. And then Ronda started calling me. First, it was just to ask me questions about school. Then she started asking me for advice about Hank. I told Lisa, and Lisa got sore. She said Ronda was after me, and she told me to tell her to stop bothering me. But I didn't. After a while, she'd come over to my house or I'd go over to hers. Just to talk. At first. About her problems with Hank. What's so funny?"

"Nothing's funny."

"So why are you laughing?"

"I guess because I'm nervous. Sometimes I laugh when I'm nervous. But go on." Lori tried to stop laughing.

"So after a while, Ronda broke up with Hank."

"You told her to?"

"No, I didn't," he said. "Not exactly."

"And I bet you broke up with Lisa."

"No, Lisa broke up with me. She was . . . she is . . . a nice girl, a very nice girl. She broke up with me, and she stopped being friends with Ronda."

"I think I like Lisa."

"Look, Lori, it's not Ronda's fault if she . . . if she really liked me. People can't help themselves, you know."

"Go on."

"Well, Ronda admitted that she'd been crazy about me for a long time. Even before we knew each other. She said she'd see me in the hall, and sometimes she'd come watch the basketball games because I was on the team."

"You play basketball, Phil?"

"Yeah. I'm not really that good. But when you're tall, people always think you should play basketball."

"How tall are you?"

"Six four."

"So go on," she said.

"Well, I wasn't sure. I mean I thought Ronda was kind of pretty and . . ."

"And?"

"Well, interesting. And I felt sorry for the trouble she was having with Hank."

"I bet you never asked Hank what he thought."

"But I wasn't sure I really liked her," Phil said. "She was different from the other girls I went out with. She seemed older and more sure of herself. And she was kind of bossy."

"So?"

"Well, at first, I couldn't make up my mind. She kept calling me and inviting me to go places with her. And I'd go, but we didn't . . . I mean we didn't really make out. But then, about a couple of months ago, I suddenly really began to care for her. For a couple of weeks, it was just great. I guess we saw each other every day, and we got in pretty deep. Then I was the one who started calling her all the time and making plans."

"So what happened?"

"I just couldn't stop thinking about her. I loved her so much. Don't laugh, Lori. What's the use? You'll laugh anyway. But I wanted to marry her. We're both only seventeen, but I wanted to get married."

"What did she say?"

"She said no."

"That's the first good thing I've heard about her," Lori said.

"And she started saying maybe we were getting too serious. Maybe we should cool it a little bit. I mean, she still loved me. That's what she said. But she thought it was getting too heavy."

"So what did you say?"

"Well, the more she talked about easing up, the more I felt I loved her. I couldn't stand it when she talked like that. I just wanted her all to myself. I didn't want to ease up. I never felt like this with anybody else. I mean, I liked Lisa, and there was a girl named Ellen Berger, who I really had a deep crush on. But it was nothing like this. I couldn't get her out of my mind."

"Look, Phil, let me ask you something."

"What?"

"Does this girl, Ronda, make you feel good?"

"I just told you, Lori, I love her."

"No, but you're not answering my question. Does she make you feel good?"

"Well—if she acted the way I wanted her to."

"Well, even when she did, Phil, did she make you feel good?"

"Yeah—she made me feel wonderful. I felt like I was on top of the world. Like I didn't have to sleep or drink or eat. . . ."

"I wouldn't like that," Lori told him.

"All I wanted to do was be with her."

"So were you happy when you were together? Did you have good times? Did you laugh a lot?"

"We couldn't take our hands off each other."

"See? That's what I mean. It was just sex. That's all. Sex isn't love." Lori made a face.

"What do you know? How much experience have you had?"

"Not much. Maybe none. I've never been in love, and I've never had sex with anybody."

"So what do you know?"

"All I need to know, Phil. There's love and there's sex. And if you're lucky, and that's what I'm going to be looking for, you get both—love and sex."

"You don't know anything."

"And I want to be happy. I think I'll know when I'm really in love, because I'll feel happy. And you're not happy with Ronda. I don't think you ever were. Even when she said she loved you."

"She still loves me," he said.

"She says she loves you?"

"Yes, she does. I spoke to her last night. I think she's coming around. She said she loved me. She said she guesses she'll always love me. She said she just needed a little space for a while. But now, maybe we should get together again like before. I think when she saw me on the beach yesterday with you . . ."

"Congratulations! I'm glad I could help you out."

"No, listen. . . ."

"And I bet she's coming to the beach today, and you want me to go join the wolf pack."

"No, no, Lori, listen. . . ."

"Look, Phil, just go away and don't talk to me. I've got my own problems, you know. You think you're the only one in this world. Like most boys. They only want to talk about themselves, but they never want to hear what you have to say. I'm sick of it. And I'm sick of you."

Lori turned the volume of her radio up so

loud that the people on the blankets around her started yelling. Phil reached over and turned it down. He looked very sad and very solemn.

"Let me ask you just one question, Lori, and then I'll go."

"What?"

"Did you make an extra egg salad sandwich today?"

Lori tried hard, but she couldn't help herself. She felt her mouth twitching, and she turned away from him. The laughter came bursting out finally. She could feel her shoulders heaving. What was the use of being angry? She turned around and faced him. He was grinning at her.

"No, I didn't make an extra egg salad sandwich. You can have half of mine if you like. But I'm not going to go sit in the sun with your friends."

"Okay, Lori, okay. It's good to see you laughing again. You really are a good sport."

"So don't ask me to go sit in the sun."

"I'm not asking you, Lori."

"Because I won't."

"It's okay, because Ronda wants to sit in the shade anyway."

Lori stood up.

"Where are you going?"

"Some place else," she told him.

"But you just said you don't want to sit in the sun. You just said . . ."

Lori unwrapped her sandwich and handed him half.

"Lori, you just said . . ."

She rolled up her beach towel and picked up her other things. She turned around and faced Phil. "I changed my mind," she told him. "I guess it's time for me to start working on my tan."

Monday

"Where have you been?"

"Oh hi, Phil. What's new? How's Ronda?"

"I've been coming here every day. I even came on my lunch hour Saturday and Sunday. Where have you been?"

"Around."

"I didn't know where you lived. You said your name was Fisher, but I didn't know how you spelled it. I looked in the phone book. Some people spell it F-i-s-h-e-r, and some people spell it F-i-s-c-h-e-r. A couple people spell it F-i-c-h-e-r, and there's even somebody who spells it F-i-s-h-c-e-r. I called that one. I figured if anybody was going to be different, it was going to be you."

Lori giggled. His face looked so grim and gloomy.

"I spell it F-i-s-h-e-r."

"And I didn't even know where you lived—Berkeley, Albany, Oakland?"

"I live in El Cerrito."

"And I bet you don't even know my name."

"Sure I know your name. It's Phil."

"Phil what?"

"Phil . . . uh . . ."

"See! You don't even know my name. And what's so funny?"

"Nothing. Nothing's funny."

"So why are you laughing? And where have you been?"

"Oh, I decided to go to Lake Temescal," she said. "It's just about as easy to get there from my house. I went there last week."

"That's a crummy place."

"I don't think so." She smiled at him.

"It's always crowded."

"It's crowded here, too."

"And there's no shade there at all."

"I don't need the shade anymore."

"You've really got a tan, Lori. You must have been sitting out in the sun all last week."

"That's right. I've been sitting out in the sun

and listening to my radio and just being laid back. It's been great. The best week I've had in ages."

"I wish I could say the same."

"Ronda been hassling you?"

"Never mind about Ronda," he said. "I want to talk about you."

"About me?"

"Yes, you, Lori. I've been thinking about you. All week I've been thinking about you, and I've been getting madder and madder."

"At me?"

"No. Not at you. At me. I guess I've been getting madder and madder at me."

"Why is that?" she asked.

"Because you were right. I did use you, and . . ."

"It's all right, Phil. Forget it. I did—long ago."

"No, it's not all right. You're a good kid. A nice girl, a kind girl."

"How do you know?" she asked.

"I can tell."

"You mean because I'm always laughing?"

"I don't know what I mean. Just shut up a minute and let me talk. And turn that damn thing down."

Lori giggled. "I guess you don't like music."

"I'm getting to hate music. Stop talking and stop laughing and LISTEN!"

"I'm listening."

"You said I was self-centered."

"No, I didn't."

"Something like it, Lori. You said I was only interested in myself. You said I'm like all boys. They only want to talk about themselves."

"That's true," Lori said.

"No, it's not."

"It is, Phil. Even my brother Tom. He's a pretty nice guy. But all he ever talks about is himself. And my father . . . well, lately he's improving. But men are like that. And maybe it's the women's fault. My mother always spoiled Tom. And she spoiled my little brother, Eddie, too."

"She didn't spoil you?" he asked.

"I guess she spoiled me, too. But it was different with me. She spoiled me in a different way. She talked to me. She talked to me about herself. But she only listened to my brothers. The way girls listen to boys. They think boys won't like them if they talk about themselves."

"Well, I'm not like that. I mean, I'm not usually like most boys. But you don't know what

I'm like. You've only seen the crummy side of me."

"Forget it, Phil."

"No, I won't forget it. I realized you knew a lot about me—about my problems with Ronda, and that I want to drop out of school and work for a TV repair shop, and that I'm working for Sugar Daddy's. You know a lot about me, but I don't know anything about you."

"You know I like egg salad."

"Yes, Lori, and that you eat soup for breakfast and don't like new things."

"Well, Phil—what else do you want to know?"

"Whatever you want to tell me."

"I don't want to tell you anything."

"Because you think I'm a jerk, Lori. Because you can't trust me. Because I took advantage of you. . . ."

"No—it's because . . . well . . . there's nothing to tell."

"Sure there is. You've been coming out to the beach for the past few weeks—maybe longer. You come all by yourself, and you stay all day. You swim, and you listen to the radio, and you lie on your beach towel in the shade. . . ."

"Not anymore."

"Okay, in the sun, and you listen to your

radio. You don't come with any friends. . . ."

"Pretty good, Sherlock Holmes." She smiled a weak little smile.

"I figure you're sixteen or so."

"I'll be seventeen in September."

"And you're not bad looking," he said.

"Thanks."

"As a matter of fact, Lori, you're good looking. You were sort of pasty looking when I first met you. But now, with your tan, you really look good."

"Anything else?" she asked.

"Well, I know you're an athlete."

"How can you tell that?"

"Well, I know you're a good swimmer. And you've got some scars on your legs which could be from skiing."

"No, I don't ski," she told him.

"Well, maybe you fell off a trampoline or some balancing bars."

"No, I didn't, and I'm not a big athlete, and, Phil, I don't want to talk about the scars on my legs."

"Because you don't trust me."

"Because I just don't want to. And why do you want to know, anyway?"

"Because I'm really interested, Lori. And because I don't want you to think I only care about myself, and . . ."

"And?"

"And because of the way you said something."

"What was that?"

"The way you said you had your own problems. Lori, you weren't laughing when you said that, and it made me feel, well . . ."

"What?"

"Well, I guess I've been thinking of you as kind of a lightweight. You know, because you laugh all the time, and you—well, you don't do anything except lie on the beach and listen to the radio. But I've been thinking about you and the way you said you had problems. I thought maybe you needed a friend who would listen to you. Maybe . . ."

"You were sorry for me, Phil?"

"Well . . ."

"Because you didn't think I had any friends?"

"Well—you always come alone," he said.

"No—I've got friends."

"That's nice."

"You don't believe me, Phil, but I do. Girl friends mostly. I never went out much with boys."

"Well, I never saw you with a girl friend either."

"I know."

"So that's why," he said gently.

"That's why you didn't think I had any friends."

"Well, yes."

"I wanted to come by myself. There's a pool close to home where most of my friends go, but I wanted to be by myself. I needed to be by myself."

"Why?"

"I have good friends, Phil. My best friend is Joanie Summers. She's the one who was with me that time in Sugar Daddy's when you gave us the double scoops."

"So why doesn't she come with you?"

"She has a job. But even if she was free, I would still come by myself."

"Why is that?"

Lori giggled.

"You can tell me, Lori. Go on."

"I . . . I've been sick."

"Sick?"

"Yes. That's why I have the scars on my legs. You really want to hear about it, Phil? It's not going to make you feel good."

"I really want to hear, Lori. Don't worry about me."

"I was in an accident in February. It was a terrible accident. It was the worst thing that ever happened to me in my whole life. Nothing that bad can ever happen to me again."

"But you're all right now, aren't you, Lori?"

"No. I'm not all right. I'm trying to be all right. But I'm not all right—yet."

"You seem all right. You're not limping or anything."

"I was in the hospital for a couple of months," she said slowly. "Both of my legs were broken, and my hip, and my wrist. There were lots of other things too, but they fixed me up. No, I'm not limping. But inside—inside, I'm limping."

"I'm sorry, Lori. What kind of an accident was it?"

"A car accident. On the Golden Gate Bridge. This car coming from the other direction, it lost control. It hit us head on. The driver was going very fast. It was horrible. I can still hear the glass breaking and the sound of horns and the crunch of bones breaking. I wake up at night sometimes, and I can hear it all, and I still scream out, and my father, my poor father, he . . ."

"Was he in the car with you?"

"No . . . but he has to come and comfort me when I wake up screaming. He has to take care of me. Sometimes I can't control myself. I wet the bed. He helps me change my sheets, and he makes me hot milk. He tries very hard. He's not used to taking care of children. He's . . . doing the best he can."

"Lori . . . Lori . . ."

"Tom is trying, too, my brother Tom. He's eighteen, in college. But he's home most weekends, and he takes me out a lot. I missed so much school last term. I guess I'll have to repeat most of the courses. But my doctor says not to worry. He says it wasn't my fault. It was the other car. I was driving, but he says there wasn't anything anybody could have done. He says this summer I should try to take it easy . . . to relax . . . to lie in the sun and not to think of anything. He says I have to try and forget. He says I have to just learn to start living again without her. He says . . ."

"Lori—who else was in the car with you?"

"My mother. She was in the car. She . . . she . . . Oh, Phil . . . I miss her so much."

Tuesday

"You know something, Phil?"

"What?"

"I'm glad we're not sitting over there in the shade anymore. Just look how mobbed it is with people. How can they stand being so jammed in together?"

"Mmm."

"You know something else, Phil?"

"What?"

"I'm glad you brought your old beach towel down today. I really like it. Much better than your new one."

"You know something, Lori?"

"What?"

"You still don't know my last name."

"I guess you think I should. I guess we really should be formally introduced. It's not fair to cry all over somebody and tell him all your troubles and not even know what his last name is."

"My name is Rivers," Phil said. And he shook her hand.

"That's a nice name." Lori giggled.

"I think so, too."

"How are your feet?"

"Black and blue."

"I'm sorry, Phil. I guess I stepped all over your feet yesterday. I couldn't stop talking. Even after we left the beach, I kept talking and stepping all over your feet."

"What kind of shoes are those, anyway?"

"They're sandal clogs. I guess the bottoms are made of wood. That's why it hurt so much when I kept stepping on your feet."

"They're so clunky, Lori."

"I like them."

"Do you ever wear regular shoes?"

"Sure I wear regular shoes, Phil. I have a pair of hiking boots, and I generally wear my Adidas to school, and I have plain clogs."

"No. I mean regular shoes. Like for going out—high-heeled shoes," he insisted.

"Me? High-heeled shoes?"

"Yes, you. Why not you?"

"I'm five ten and he wants to know if I wear high-heeled shoes. Are you kidding! If I wore high-heeled shoes, I'd be over six feet."

"So what's so terrible about that, Lori?"

"For a girl?"

"They look pretty."

"You mean sexy."

"Well, yes—sexy—and pretty."

"That's not the way I think of myself," she said. "Anyway, I'm too tall to wear high-heeled shoes. You can't walk in them, anyway. They're only to show off in—to attract bird-brain boys like . . ."

"Like me?"

"If the shoe fits." Lori giggled. "That's a pretty good one, isn't it?"

"No, it isn't."

"I bet Ronda wears high-heeled shoes."

"Yes, she does. She has a pair of black ones. There's hardly any shoe, and her toes stick out, and there's a strap across the ankle. Mmm—I love those shoes." Phil rolled his eyes.

"You would. But . . . but . . . yesterday I didn't ask you about Ronda. What's happening with Ronda?"

"Nothing much."

"Well . . . are you . . . ?"

"We were, Lori. We tried for a while last week. But then she said she wasn't ready to get into a real deep relationship with me or anybody else. She said she needed time."

"And what did you say?"

"I agreed with her."

"You changed your mind?" Lori asked.

"I guess I did. Suddenly I just got tired of the whole thing. I got tired of feeling so heavy all the time. It's like you said—I want to feel good. And lately, I haven't been feeling so good."

"You'll be all right, Phil."

"I know. And Lori . . ."

"What?"

"You'll be all right, too."

"I guess I will. I'm trying. And I guess I have to thank you, Phil."

"You mean for listening yesterday?"

"No—for making me so mad last week."

"Oh, that! I'd rather not remember that."

"No, it was good. It made me feel alive again. These past few months, all I could think about was the accident. Nothing else mattered. And then I met you on the beach, and you made me sore. So I went to another beach, and I kept thinking about you and Ronda."

"Oh god!"

"And I wanted to know what happened. I was curious. For the first time in months, I was curious about somebody else. You see, I was really the self-centered one. But finally, it was like being alive again. I wanted to know what happened to you and Ronda. That's why I came back."

"Lori . . . I think you and I . . ."

"I don't know, Phil."

"Damn it, Lori, you don't even know what I was going to say."

Lori giggled.

"So just listen to me and shut up. I was just going to say I'd like to get to know you better."

"Phil, I need a lot of time. You know, I'm still not able to drive in a car. I take buses, and I haven't been able to go across any bridges. I'm still not over it. I don't know if I'll ever be completely over it."

"Oh, you will. I know you will."

"Thanks, Phil. You're a good friend."

"And I'm going to help you."

"How?"

"Well, first, I'm going to go shopping with you and help you pick out a decent pair of shoes."

"If you mean a pair with high heels, you can forget it. I hate the way they look, and I hate the way they feel, and I don't need to be any taller than I am."

"You're too short for me. High heels will bring you closer to my size. I don't like short women."

"But Ronda . . ."

"Who's Ronda? And then I think it's time you learned to eat properly. Today I brought some lunch for you. I'm tired of eating your sandwiches, so I decided it's time you tried mine."

"It's very nice of you, Phil, but I really like my own sandwiches best."

"How do you know you won't like mine, if you won't even try?"

"Okay, Phil, I'll try. What is it?"

He was holding out a sandwich towards her, and she took it, looked at it, and giggled.

"You know, Lori, you've got a sexy giggle."

"Just shut up, Phil, and eat," she told him. And she bit into the egg salad and peanut butter sandwich he had made for her.